This is My Book

Name _____

Date _____

This is the third in a series of Storybooks for Little Folks published by Deere & Company and distributed by John Deere dealerships throughout North America. The first two books, JOHNNY TRACTOR AND HIS PALS and CORNY CORNPICKER FINDS A HOME, were published originally in 1958. They were reprinted in 1988 in response to literally hundreds of requests from parents who read these books as a child and wanted to share them with their children or grandchildren.

printed on recycled paper

Family Reunion

A JOHN DEERE STORYBOOK FOR LITTLE FOLKS

From a story by Lois and J.R. Hobbs and Kris Carr
Illustrated by Roy A. Bostrom, Retired Staff Artist, John Deere

In an old shed on Bob Fowler's farm, there were a lot of old farm tractors that hadn't been used for a long, long time. Though it was warm and dry inside, there was dust all over everything. And big cobwebs hung in the corner.

The tractors were all good friends. When they were alone they talked and visited among themselves, just like people do.

Wally, the old Waterloo Boy Tractor, usually started the conversations. He liked to talk about the "old times" on the Fowler farm.

"I was the first tractor Grandpa Fowler ever had," Wally would say, proudly. "He was just a young man back in 1923 when he brought me home. I hadn't been here very long before Grandpa Fowler put me to work running the threshing machine in the oat field.

He and I worked a lot of hot summer days threshing oats. He needed lots of oats for his horses. The neighbors used to come by and watch me work. Then they would ask Grandpa Fowler if he'd bring me over to their farms and help them with their threshing. I was glad to do it."

Donald, the Model "D" Tractor stood next to Wally. He was low and strong with big yellow wheels with iron lugs. He had a steel seat and a beautiful set of fenders. He liked to brag about the number of acres he could plow in a day.

"One day, back in 1930, Grandpa Fowler started me up just as the sun was coming up and when we quit that night we had plowed 15 acres! I remember lots of times he would take me to the county fair to enter me in a plowing match. I won a lot of trophies for him. They are up in the big house in a nice case," he told them all.

Across the way was a Model "A" Tractor. His name was Ace.
He was sleek and trim. Grandpa Fowler had let his son, Bob,
run him and help with the cultivating.

"Bob was just a teenager when he first started running me,"
Ace said smiling as he remembered those days. "We cultivated
corn and beans, acre after acre.

He never had to stop and give me a rest like he did with the horses. The horses used to stand in the pasture and whinney at us as we went past. I think they were really glad that they didn't have to work so hard in the heat and the bitey flies anymore. Bob was sure a good tractor operator. He always kept me clean and greased and put away in the shed at night."

In another corner was a little Model "M" Tractor. He didn't like his real name so everyone called him "Mitey". He was small, but he could do so many things that no one ever made fun of him for being smaller than the rest.

When one of the tractors would ask him about some of the things he used to do for Grandpa Fowler and Bob, he would say

in his quiet, proud little voice, "Well, I mowed the hay and the roadside ditches. I moved lots of snow and dirt with the blade they put on the front of me. I plowed the garden for Grandpa Fowler and planted sweet corn. One time, Bob Fowler entered me in a tractor pull with lots of other tractors my size and I out-pulled them all!"

Summers and winters came and went for a lot of years. Then, one day, the big door opened and let in a bright stream of sunlight. A little boy and an old man stepped in. The little boy asked, "What's in here, Grandpa?"

Grandpa Fowler stood looking at all the old tractors. He remembered using them when he was a young man. "Did you really use all these old tractors, Grandpa?" the little boy asked.

"I sure did, Tad. It was a long time ago, your Dad and I farmed lots of years with them. It was hard work but they did a good job. When the new tractors came along we just put the old timers out here to give them a well-deserved rest." "Won't we ever use them again, Grandpa?" Tad asked. "You bet! Your Dad and I are taking the old tractors to Waterloo, Iowa and show them off. There's going to be a family reunion just for old tractors...but first we've got to clean them up a little," Grandpa Fowler told Tad.

"They sure have a lot of dust on them, Grandpa."

"They will look just great when we spruce them up," Grandpa Fowler said. "You can help me. And if your Dad says it's okay, you can go to Waterloo with us."

Grandpa and Tad and Tad's Dad soon came back with lots of old rags, soap and water and paint and brushes. They washed dirt away and added a little green or yellow paint where it was needed. The old tractors began to shine and twinkle. They looked at each other with pride when they saw how good everyone looked.

When they were all done, Bob Fowler backed up the semi-truck and started loading up all the tractors very carefully. They all waved goodbye to the new tractors, who weren't going.
"Goodbye!" they hollered. "We're going to Waterloo! We're going to a family reunion!"

At Waterloo, the old tractors looked around with amazement at all the tractors that looked just like them! There were people selling parts and toys and all sorts of interesting things. It was like a farm show and state fair rolled into one!

Grandpa Fowler's tractors drew a lot of attention because they were in such good shape and so well taken care of. They were very proud when people came along and yelled, "Hey, look at these great old timers!"

After a few, exciting days it was time to go home. The reunion was over.

All the way home, the old tractors talked about the wonderful time they had. "Do you suppose we will ever go again?" asked Mitey.

Wally, who was the oldest, said, "Yes, we will probably go again, sometime. It will be something to look forward to."

Ace, the Model "A" said, "I can't wait to tell all our friends about the things we've seen. Do you think they will believe us?" Donald, the old Model "D" said, "Sure they'll believe us. If they don't I'll make them believe it," he boasted. He was always so proud of being so strong. They all laughed at him and then were silent all the way home.

It was quiet in the old shed again. All the tractors were back in their places. The dust had begun to settle down on them again. The old tractors had told their friends all about Waterloo and the family reunion. They all thought their own thoughts about old times and new times and the things they had done. They were very content to be snug and dry and to rest in the old shed on Farmer Fowler's farm.